For anyone who's ever dreamed of making something.
Let your thoughts become ideas and let your ideas
become creations.
—L.R. & J.R.

ISBN 978-0-06-240360-5

The artists used polymer clay, acrylic paint, spray paint, sandpaper, tissue paper, a macro lens, oil paint, dental floss, coffee grounds, sugar packs, caulk, recycled cardboard, foam, hair, glue, cloth, paper, flowers, wire, wood, sticks, turf, rocks, resin clay, felt, gum wrappers, wood varnish, ribbon, chalk pastels, colored pencil, aluminum foil, tape, and crayons to create the illustrations for this book.
The pillow that appears on page 19 was created by
Derek Sanchez-Hoeksema of Oh Sew Nerdy.
Typography by Erin Fitzsimmons

18 19 20 21 22 SCP 10 9 8 7 6 5 4 3 2 1

❖

First Edition

Sweet

Let's do this!

By
Liz and
Jimmy
Reed

Success

HARPER
An Imprint of HarperCollinsPublishers

Sprinkle Dee Scoops loved to make things.
She whipped up any project that came to mind.

Starting a new project was fun.
Finishing it was something else.

Scoops was in the middle of so many projects that she forgot to complete the most important one of all.

You're invited to the

Cherry Twins' Surprise Birthday Bash.

Saturday at 2 p.m.
Please bring homemade gifts.

DO NOT BE LATE.

We don't want to spoil
the surprise!

-Waffle

Her present wasn't close to being done,
and the party was today!

If Scoops was late, she'd miss the big surprise.

She scrambled to finish the present in time.

The painting was still wet as Scoops dashed out the door.

By the time she arrived, the surprise was over.

SURPRISE!

The cherry twins were gushing over everyone's handmade goodies. Scoops glanced at her gift and froze.

The painting was a wet, gooey mess.

Scoops just wanted to go home,

but she was so upset that she missed her turn.

Now headed the wrong way,
Scoops had no idea where she was going.

Then Scoops heard cheering.

Soon her cold thoughts from the party melted away.

Well, there's no turning back now.

And she finally saw the end was in sight.

Scoops crossed the finish line and shouted with glee.

Completing the race made Scoops
remember what she loved most.

No time for rest!

Starting a project was fun,

but finishing it was something else.

I love it so much!

I love it more!

Scoops' love for finishing things didn't stop there.

She told her friends about her biggest project yet.

And together they all helped Scoops
finish what she had started.